The Young Collector's
Illustrated Classics

By
Jules Verne

Adapted by
Diane Flynn Grund

Copyright © 1994 Masterwork Books
A Division of Kidsbooks, Inc.
3535 West Peterson Avenue
Chicago, IL 60659

Manufactured in the United States of America

Contents

Chapter

1

The Monster at Sea

It was in the year 1886 that the monster was first seen. Sailors from every country who dared to challenge the high seas, trembled when night fell over the great oceans. The stories that the sailors told were different from ship to ship, but on one point they all agreed: the monster was huge—gigantic!

The monster was said to be two hundred feet long! And there were some old seamen who swore it was a mile long and three miles wide!

On black, moonless nights, sailors would spot a strange glow in the distance. It lit up the water. The men would then lie

awake all night, shaking in their bunks.

As word of the monster spread everywhere, scientists from all over the world
began to wonder what it was that roamed
the dark oceans.

What was this creature? People everywhere wanted to know. A year had passed since the first sighting of this mysterious monster. Everyone expected the scientists to solve this problem—as soon as possible!

The governments of many countries were becoming very worried as fear of the monster grew. The great men of science met together, arguing far into many

nights. But they could find no answer. Out at sea, the monster still prowled the cold ocean depths.

One chilly evening at sea, a very fast and powerful steamer, the *Scotia*, was sailing the grey waters of the North Atlantic. All of a sudden there was a terrible jolt.

On board the *Scotia* it had been peaceful. It was dusk, and nearly time for

dinner. Passengers were coming to eat in the great salon.

Up on deck, the sailors on the evening watch had taken their posts. Suddenly, the dreaded lights appeared on the darkening sea. The sailors froze and looked at one another in terror.

"It's the monster! Run and warn the captain!" Their frightened voices trembled. But just as quickly as they came, the lights vanished. The crewmen wiped their sweaty faces and relaxed.

Then it happened. The *Scotia* was struck with the force! Panic broke out in the salon. Tables, dishes, and people were thrown to the floor.

Captain Anderson was rushing about trying to calm the frightened guests, when a sailor from the engine room ran in.

"We're sinking!" he cried. His face was white with horror.

People began to rush in all directions; the slower ones were knocked to the floor. The ship was in total confusion!

The captain climbed onto a table and

tried to get the attention of the running crowd.

"Stop it! All of you!" he commanded in a firm voice. Slowly, the passengers began to quiet down and, at last, there was order on board the *Scotia*.

The captain led the crew below deck to see how bad the damage was. What they found frightened even the brave Captain Anderson.

Icy sea water was gushing in and

quickly flooding the forward hold. The leak was very bad.

A brave sailor dove down under the ship to find out the size of the leak. When he was at last pulled back on deck, he had alarming news.

"There is a hole in the hull at least

seven feet in diameter!" he reported, as he stood dripping and shivering in front of the captain.

There was no doubt, the *Scotia* was in terrible danger. If the water that was pouring in from the hole reached the engine room, the ship would go straight to the bottom of the cold Atlantic! The *Scotia* had no choice but to make her way over three hundred miles back to port.

After three days, the injured ship finally docked safely in England. Experts from all over came to look at the hole in the Scotia to try to figure out what could have made it.

They were all shocked by what they saw: the hole in the ship was cut so neatly that it looked as though it had been done by some kind of razor-sharp cutting machine. And it was made through several inches of solid iron!

Everyone was asking the same question: what sort of creature could have made that hole? No one knew the answer, but one thing was clear: no ship was safe at sea!

It was at this time that I came into the story. The creature had become the terror of the seas, and I was determined to hunt it down. My name is Professor Pierre Aronnax. The French government sent me to see what could be done about this monster. So, I came to New York with my faithful servant, Conseil.

Soon I met the bold and famous

Captain Farragut. It was on his ship that we were going to sail in our search for the monster. He would be in charge of the sailing, and I would be in charge of the searching. Together, we would make that creature run for its life!

Our ship was called the *Abraham Lincoln*. It was one of the fastest ships ever built.

The day came for us to leave on our great search. Crowds had gathered on the docks to see us off. There were many flags waving, and brightly colored streamers floated on the soft breeze. A band played, and we were even given a twenty-one-gun salute! I was sorry to have to leave, but it was time to cast off. We headed out to sea, while thousands of people cheered.

Conseil and I stood on deck watching the shore become smaller and smaller in the distance. He looked a bit homesick, and I wanted to cheer him up.

"There's nothing to be frightened of, my boy," I promised him. "I have a pretty good idea just what we're looking for."

"You do?" asked Conseil, quite surprised.

"Yes, I think it is a very large type of whale, called a narwhal," I whispered. "This whale has a long, sharp horn and lives in the deepest parts of the ocean. The

ships going by have most likely disturbed it and made it angry. Just think what a discovery like this will mean to science!" I concluded happily.

Conseil looked better. "Only a whale," he laughed.

We stood looking at the dancing waves. If only we had known then what was to happen!

Chapter

2

The Hunt Begins

The crew of the *Abraham Lincoln* was as bold and fearless as their captain. They were not afraid of the creature and were glad to have the chance to hunt it down. Captain Farragut had promised a reward of two thousand dollars to the first man to spot the monster. The sailors didn't have to be told twice to keep their eyes open!

One of the crew became a close friend of mine. His name was Ned Land, and he was, by far, the most powerful man on board. Ned was in charge of the deadly harpoons on the ship. If anyone could fight the monster—it was Ned!

He knew a lot about the sea and the many forms of life that swam in it. But to my surprise, he was the only one who did not believe in the monster!

Days went by, and we saw no sign of the creature. We had sailed all the way down to South America, around its south-ernmost tip, and we had now reached the great Pacific Ocean.

We stared at the sparkling waves so hard that we nearly went blind looking for the beast! We saw nothing but calm, blue water.

By this time everyone was getting tired of the search, and some were even beginning to wonder if there really was a monster.

Only Conseil and I kept believing. But Ned Land kept looking at the sea as if he were expecting something to rise up from the deep.

Then came the cry that sent all hands racing to their posts. It was Ned shouting, "Ahoy, there it is! Off the leeward bow!"

It was there in the water, the creature

we had come so far to see. It was a dark night. The sky and water were very black, but I had no trouble spotting the monster. Up from the depths of the ocean came a blinding light. We saw the gigantic shape of what looked like a whale—only bigger!

"Sir, the creature glows!" cried Conseil, as he leaned over the railing to get a better look.

"It must be some kind of electric whale," I told him. "You've heard of electric eels, haven't you?"

"Yes indeed!" Conseil exclaimed loudly, "I've also heard that they can give you a nasty shock! Imagine what a creature *this* size could do!"

Captain Farragut rushed forward, "Five hundred dollars to the man who can spear that beast!" he yelled.

An old, grey sailor stepped to the gun. The harpoon gun fired with a mighty blast. The deadly spear hit the beast—but bounced off!

"What the devil is that creature made of, solid iron?" cursed the old gunner.

Before anyone had a chance to say anything, the monster suddenly headed straight for the *Abraham Lincoln*! Everyone held his breath. Then just as suddenly, the creature's lights went out and it seemed to vanish.

"It's playing games with us," muttered the brave Captain Farragut.

Then, in the darkness, I could hear a loud hiss not far away from the ship.

"That's the sound that a whale makes when it spouts water," said Ned, "only this is much louder!"

Then the creature appeared again a little ahead of the ship. It seemed to be almost waiting for us. We followed it through the long night; everyone was too excited to get any sleep.

Finally, daylight came and the monster's light again disappeared, but we could still see its huge, dark shape as it slipped through the water.

"Now's our chance!" yelled Ned. "Let's get that blasted thing once and for all!"

"Engines full ahead!" ordered Farragut. "I'll go after that beast until my ship blows up!" The chase was on!

We soon found out that the creature was much faster than we had thought. As soon as we sped up, so did the monster. We had all we could do to keep up with it.

All that day we chased the beast. We followed the glowing trail that it left in the water. Captain Farragut stood muttering at the rail.

"Confound that animal!" he cursed. "I've never seen anything move that fast!"

"Our only hope is that we can tire it out," I said, feeling pretty tired myself.

But the monster kept right on going. Night came and still we followed the beast.

Then the creature disappeared again. We couldn't see anything on the dark sea.

Time passed, and I began to worry that the hunt was over. Just as we were about to give up, the brilliant light appeared way off in the distance.

Slowly, we moved toward it. The beast seemed to be standing still. Then we were right next to it! The glow was dazzling under the water. We could hear its loud breathing.

Then I saw Ned Land. He crept up to the beast. His sharpest harpoon was in his hand.

"This is it!" he hissed. He raised the harpoon. The harpoon flew straight for the mark. As it struck the monster, there was a ringing sound—as if the beast were made of metal!

At once, the creature's light went out. And just as quickly, two powerful streams

of water shot out of the monster and swept across the ship. There was a terrible bump. I lost my balance, falling headfirst into the dark sea.

Now I was in a terrible fix! As soon as I could float, I looked up towards the ship.

Someone must have seen me go over. But the *Abraham Lincoln* was moving away in the darkness!

"Help! Help!" I cried, choking.

I was sure that I was lost now. When the ship left, so did my hope for rescue. My wet clothes were clinging to me, making it very hard to swim. I tried my best to stay afloat, but before long, I was too tired to move.

I knew I was drowning! I could not breathe! I tried to cry out for help one last time, but my mouth filled with water, and I began to sink. Then the dark water closed over my head.

Just as I had given my life up to the sea, I felt something grab my clothes, and I was pulled up to the surface. I could hardly believe my eyes! It was my dear, faithful servant, Conseil!

"If you'll hold onto me Professor, I think you will find it easier to stay afloat," said Conseil quite calmly. I clung to his strong arm.

As soon as I could get my breath, I

turned to him, 'Were you swept overboard at the same time as I?" I asked him.

"No sir," he replied, "I jumped over. You are my master, and it was my duty to follow you."

"No man ever had a better servant— or a finer friend," I told him.

Silently, we drifted in the icy waves.

Our wet clothes felt heavy; it seemed as if they were made of lead. Conseil had a knife, and we cut some of them off. That made swimming easier. To save our strength, one of us would swim and hold up the other; then we would switch places. By taking turns, we hoped we could hold out until morning. The ship would surely be able to spot us in daylight. It was our only hope!

Hour after hour went by as we tried to keep from sinking in the churning waves. We were both doing our best, but it seemed as if morning would never come! I knew I couldn't hold out much longer.

I began to get terrible cramps in my stomach. My arms and legs were stiff from

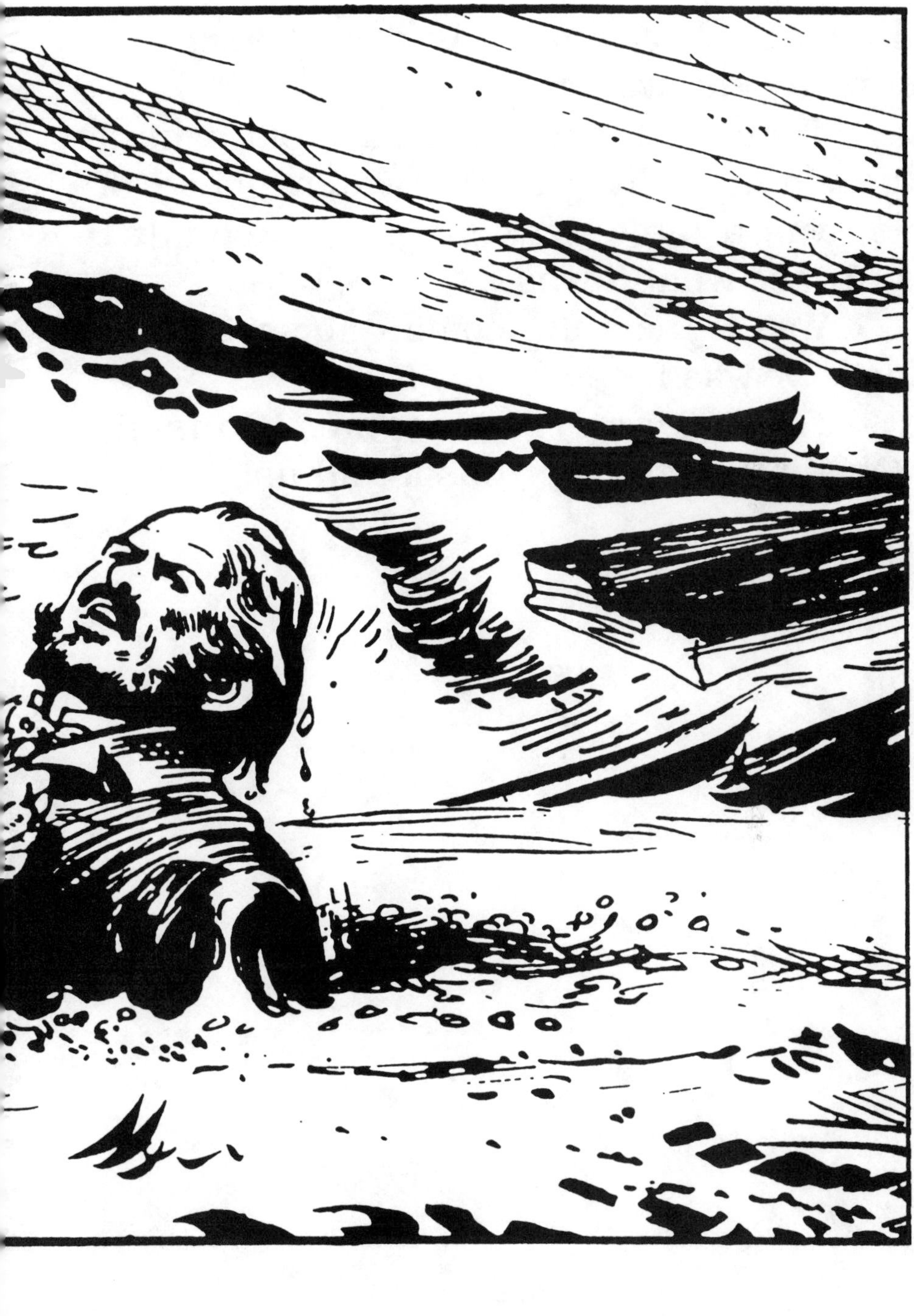

the cold. I began to go under again. I was sure my end was near!

Then the moon came out from behind the clouds. There in the water, ahead of us, was a large dark shape. We couldn't quite see what it was.

Was it the ship, coming to save us at last? Or was it . . .?

"The *monster*!" screamed Conseil. "Oh, sir, the monster has found us!"

Chapter

3

Inside the Monster

we find out what it is we're sitting
aid.

now knew that the so-called mon-
as not even alive! This *thing* that
ared the whole world was made of
t was made by men. But who?

ddenly, there was a bubbling

I hardly heard the scream of poor Conseil, because I had fainted. This time I did not expect to be saved. It was too bad that I would never get to study the monster—I was about to be eaten by it!

The next thing I knew, I was waking up. Someone was pushing on my chest to get the water out. Soon I was able to breathe more easily.

"Conseil, Conseil . . . ," I moaned.

"I'm here sir," he replied, sounding quite alive.

Before I had time to figure anything out, I saw another person standing in the moonlight.

"Why, Ned! Ned Land!" I cried in delight. "How did you? What on earth...?"

"Take it easy, Professor," Ned whispered.

By now, I had quite awakened. At least I knew one thing for certain—we were *not* in the belly of the creature! I could see the moonlight shining on the waves.

"Where is the monster?" I asked Conseil.

"We are sitting on it, sir," he replied calmly.

"This is no time for jokes!" I scolded angrily.

when
on!" I s

I
ster w
had s
steel! I
S

"He's not joking," sa
I rapped my knuck
shiny thing we were sitti

"Good heavens! It
steel!" I said in surprise.
it?"

"This is your monst
...or whatever you w
Professor," Ned answerec
also, but I was lucky. I f
hold on to," he explained

"Well, we'll see just

sound at the end of it. Then it began to move very slowly through the water.

"As long as it keeps moving *above* water, we'll be all right," said Ned. He sounded scared. "But if it decides to *dive*, we're done for!"

Conseil and I both knew he was right! Since we knew it had an engine, we knew that there had to be a crew inside. It could not run by itself !

We searched, but we could not find any way to get inside of it. Then it began to go faster and faster. Before long, it was going so fast that we could hardly hold on! Huge waves splashed up on both sides. We were not only getting soaked–we were going to fall off!

Luckily, Ned found a large, iron ring that was attached to the steel. We all held on to it. Soon after, the long night came to an end.

When the sun rose, I was able to get a better look at what we were riding on. It was large and long. It looked like a gigantic, metal fish. It had to be an amazing ship since it could go underwater. I had never seen anything like it before.

Then the worst happened! The "ship" started to dive. We would be dragged under and drowned!

"A thouand devils!" cursed Ned.

Ned, in his fright, began kicking at the steel and yelling at the top of his lungs. All at once, the ship stopped diving. There was a loud noise—like metal bolts sliding. Then a hatch opened, and a strange shape appeared. A minute later, eight huge men came out. Their faces were hidden by dark hoods. Without saying one word, they dragged us down into their strange, metal ship!

I heard the clang of an iron door closing us in. I had never been in a place so dark! We felt around and found that we were locked in a small cell.

Ned became angry. He started yelling loudly.

"A thousand devils!" he cried. "Let us out of here, you cannibals!"

"Ned, calm down! Please!" I begged. "Do you want to get us into more trouble?"

Then we were suddenly blinded by a bright light. When we could see again, there were two men standing in front of our cell. One looked very brave and strong. His eyes seemed to look right into my mind—as if he knew what I was thinking. We tried to speak to them, but they didn't seem to understand. They spoke to each other in a strange language. Then they left.

Later, a masked man brought us some food and clothes. We were hungry and gobbled it down! We were resting, when Ned became very upset again. He began to scream and bang on the bars. When a guard came to see what was wrong—Ned attacked him!

He grabbed the guard and threw him to the floor. Then he began to choke him!

Conseil tried to pull Ned's hands away from the guard's throat, but he could not break that deadly hold. The guard was gasping for air, and his face turned bright red.

Just then, a deep voice ordered Ned to let the guard go.

"Mr. Land! I would stop right now if I were you!" It was the captain—the man with those strange eyes whom we had seen before.

Whether it was the powerful voice or

the look in the captain's dark eyes I'll never know, but Ned froze like a statue!

The captain could have spoken to us before! I wondered why he hadn't. Then he said something that really surprised me.

"I know who you are, Professor Aronnax!" He sounded angry. "I also know why you and your two friends have come."

"It was by accident that we ended up

on your ship," I tried to tell him.

"Nonsense!" he snorted. "You and your friends on the *Abraham Lincoln* were trying to hunt me down—and destroy me!"

"Yes," I agreed, "but we thought that you were some kind of sea monster!" *"I am Captain Nemo!"* he roared, "and you are on board the submarine, *Nautilus*!" His eyes snapped like black fire. "You wanted to find me, and you have! Now you will be sorry that you did!"

He pulled out a gun and stood facing us.

Captain Nemo stood glaring at us. I was too afraid to argue with him. I had never heard of a ship that could go underwater. I decided to ask him what country he was from.

"I am from no country!" Nemo snapped. "I am a free man, and now I am the master of the seas! You are my prisoners!" he snarled. "If you try to escape, I will kill you!" Then he turned and walked quickly away, leaving us alone in our prison.

Chapter

4

The Nautilus

I must say that after Nemo left us, we were a very sad group! Ned paced around the tiny cell saying over and over, "I *must* get out of here!"

I was about to tell him to calm down, when Nemo came back and stood looking at us. Ned became very quiet.

I looked at Captain Nemo. His face was calm, and he seemed much kinder. "You may be prisoners, but at least I gave you a chance to live," he said softly. "I didn't have to save you from the sea, I could have let you drown," he went on to remind us.

"Will you ever let us go?" pleaded

Ned. "I've got a sweetheart waiting for me at home," he said sadly.

"I'm very sorry," said Nemo, "but you will never see your loved ones again."

When I saw the sadness in poor Ned's eyes, I was afraid my own heart would break for him.

Then Nemo clapped his hands together and gave us a big friendly smile.

"Come now, gentlemen!" he laughed. "It won't be all that bad. I promise you. This ship is very comfortable."

With that, he let Ned and Conseil out of the cell. A servant came to lead them to comfortable rooms. Then Captain Nemo asked me to come and have lunch with him.

I was led to a beautiful dining room with drapes made of fine silk and glasses of sparkling crystal. I couldn't believe my eyes. The ship was like a palace under the sea.

When I sat down, I was even more shocked to see that the plates we were to dine from were *solid* gold!

The food was quite tasty, and there was plenty of it. I asked Captain Nemo what we were eating.

"Sliced sea turtle and dolphin liver. My cook fixes it just right!" the captain exclaimed.

It sounded awful to me, but I had to agree—it did taste delicious!

After lunch, Captain Nemo showed me another beautiful room. It was his

library, full of volumes and volumes of books!

I picked books off of the shelves and looked through them. I was very pleased with the volumes he had chosen for his library. Captain Nemo seemed pleased with my approval.

20,000 Leagues Under the Sea

"This is also a smoking room," Captain Nemo said proudly. "Have a cigar, Professor?" It was the best I had ever tasted!

"That cigar is made of seaweed," Nemo said.

Then he opened the door to another room! It was filled with treasures from the sea and was even more lovely than the other rooms. There were giant shells from deep in the ocean. One huge clamshell was big enough to take a bath in! Large

pearls of many colors shone from clear cases made of crystal. Bright jewels and shiny gold coins filled box after box!

Captain Nemo must have been one of the richest men in the world! I kept wondering why he chose to live under the sea.

"I call this room my museum," said Nemo.

"It must be one of the best on this earth!" I said, unable to hide the wonder in my voice.

"These treasures are just keepsakes of a world that I have left behind," said Nemo.

"You see Professor," he said, "to the rest of the world, I am a dead man!"

"What do you mean?" I asked him.

But Captain Nemo suddenly became very quiet, so I did not try to find out any more.

Then the captain perked up again and smiled, "Would you like to see the engine room?"

"Indeed I would!" I said cheerfully.

Captain Nemo again led the way. We

walked to the very back of the *Nautilus*.
Finally, we got to the big, steel door of the
engine room.

Then I saw the mighty engine that
ran this great ship. I could hardly believe
the size of it! It was at least sixty-five feet
long!

I stood looking at the huge engine,

while Nemo told me how it worked. He said that the whole ship was run by electricity made from sea water. If Captain Nemo would only tell his secrets to the rest of the world! But somehow, I knew he would not.

"You must be very proud of your ship," I said.

"I love it as a father loves his own child," he replied with shining eyes.

We left the engine room and went back to the "museum." Ned and Conseil were there waiting for us.

"I have something to show you," the captain said. Suddenly the lights went out. It was very black! We waited, a little afraid.

Then the whole wall slid open, and we saw the bottom of the sea. Only the glass was between us and the creatures of the deep! We could see a giant squid looking right at us—and he looked *hungry!*

"There is no need to be afraid," said Nemo, "the glass is as strong as steel."

We stood looking at a sight more

beautiful than any that we had seen on earth! The water was lit up, and it sparkled like a million blue diamonds. Fish of all sizes darted through the shining bubbles. There were bright reds and blazing yellows. Some creatures had their own lights that glowed gently inside of them.

I had never seen such a wonderful sight. It was like one hugh fishbowl! I

turned to say something to Captain Nemo,
but he was gone. He had left without saying a word.

I was led to my small, but comfortable cabin. Captain Nemo did not come
for me, even though it was time for dinner;
I ate alone in my room. I was sitting and
smoking another seaweed cigar, when
Nemo came to wish me good night.

I had been thinking that someone

else besides the men on board must know about the Nautilus. After all, it must have been built on land. *Someone* must have seen it! Maybe we could be rescued!

Trying to sound calm, I asked the captain where the *Nautilus* had been built.

"She was built on a lonely island far out in the middle of the ocean," Nemo answered.

"Where is this island?" I asked, still hoping.

"I blew it to bits!" he snapped. "No one must ever find me, or *you!*" he laughed.

Chapter

5

On the Ocean Floor

During the next few days, I did not see one sign of Captain Nemo. Then, one of his servants brought me a note from him. He wanted to know if I would like to go for a hunt in the forests of a nearby island. Land! A chance to go ashore— maybe a chance to escape!

Ned, Conseil, and I went down to the engine room to meet the captain. Nemo told us that we would not be going on land at all. The forests were under the sea!

We all felt angry because we had wanted to see land again. Ned was especially angry, and he refused to go with us on the hunt. Nemo helped Conseil and me

into special suits. With these suits, we could walk and breathe on the ocean floor.

Nemo gave us guns that would kill almost anything. The guns had electric bullets that would blow up when they hit—just like lightning when it strikes!

Soon a hatch slid open, and we

stepped out into a watery world! It was so easy to walk and move under the water. Our bodies were very light, so we had weights on our shoes to keep us from floating away from each other.

I saw sights even more wonderful than those I had seen through the big window of the ship. Now we could even reach out and touch things—if we dared! There were lovely flowers growing under the sea, fish, shells, and coral of dazzling colors.

We were not down very deep, and the sun was shining through the water. To my surprise, a rainbow came and lit up the sea with brilliance.

We were going down, deeper and deeper. The light blue color of the water slowly got darker. Finally, we were down to a depth of 450 feet! It was very dark. Captain Nemo switched on a light that he carried on his belt. The rest of us did the same.

We had come to a wall of solid rock, rising up from the floor of the sea. It was

the underwater part of the island. Nemo would not let us go on.

We started back to the *Nautilus*. Suddenly, Nemo grabbed onto me and pushed me down! I thought that he was trying to kill me! But Nemo lay flat on the sandy bottom—and so did Conseil.

Two huge sharks were circling above us! I held my breath as one came close. Its rough skin brushed my bare hand. Then

the great fish swam away. When I looked at my hand, it shocked me to discover that my skin had been scraped right off!

Quickly, we went back to the *Nautilus*.

A few days later, I was sitting alone and looking out the window. One of Nemo's men had bandaged my hand, and it was healing nicely.

Captain Nemo came in. I greeted him, but he didn't answer. When I spoke to him again, he acted as if I weren't even there.

The captain stood at the window. On the floor of the ocean, his men were gath-

ering fish. They just swept the fish up in big nets. They could bring in one thousand pounds of seafood in one day. We surely wouldn't starve!

Captain Nemo turned from the window and smiled. "This is living!" he boomed in his powerful voice. "This is the only life!"

I looked out at the blue water, the big catch, and wondered: was Captain Nemo right?

The next day, several of us went out for another walk. This time, Ned came with us. Even he was happy walking through the clear water.

Then we saw something that made us jump back in terror! There was a giant, black shape in the water. At first, I thought it might be a whale. Then...

"It's a ship!" I tried to yell through my mask.

It was a ship, alright. But a ship that had sunk to its doom! It looked like it had gone down only a few hours before. There on the deck of that unlucky ship was a very gruesome sight. The bodies of those who had drowned lay caught in the wreckage. Their dead captain still stood holding the wheel; he looked as if he were still

steering his ghost ship under the dark waves!

In the next few days, we saw a lot of ships rotting on the ocean floor. Big can-

nons, chains, and anchors rusted in the
dark currents. The bones of many poor
sailors also rested in this graveyard on the
sea floor.

We were moving through the Evil
Channel, in the South Pacific. These were

dangerous waters, full of jungle islands and tricky tides. Sharp coral reefs reached out like giant hands, ready to catch us.

All at once, I felt a terrible jolt. Then I heard a loud, crunching noise. The *Nautilus* had struck a reef! The ship was stuck in this terrible place! I wondered what Captain Nemo would do now?

I rushed down to the engine room. There was the captain, looking calm and cool.

"We are stuck on this reef!" I exclaimed. "What are we going to do now?"

"Do not worry, my dear Professor," Nemo said to me. "There will soon be a full moon."

"Yes, I know that!" I shouted. "So what!"

Captain Nemo explained that the moon would raise the tide, and the ship would float off the reef to safety. When he told me that, I felt foolish for not having thought of it myself.

We were near a large island, and Ned wanted fresh meat. He asked the captain if we could go ashore to hunt. To our surprise, Nemo let us go!

We were given a small boat, and in it we headed to the island. As we rowed, we enjoyed finally being above the ocean's surface. We gazed at the sky and breathed in salty air, feeling a cool breeze all the while touch our skin. It was like a wonderful dream.

After a while rowing, we landed on a sandy beach. We were so glad to see land, that we tripped over each other in our hurry to leave the boat!

"Land! Land! Good, old, solid earth!" laughed Ned.

We all danced a little jig and acted wonderfully silly for a few minutes. Then it was time to go about the serious business of finding fresh food.

It was a lovely island with sparkling waterfalls and graceful palms. A thick, green jungle began at the edge of the beach.

Besides being beautiful, the island was rich with food. We walked through the jungle, filling our sacks with fruits and vegetables.

There were coconuts, bananas, pineapples, and ripe, juicy mangoes—the sweetest fruit I had ever tasted. The island was like a marvelous dream!

After we had rested a little while, we were ready to hunt for meat. It did not take too long before Ned shot a wild pig. Then Conseil brought down a dozen fat pigeons. Soon, we had gathered all the food we needed.

We walked along, smelling the scents of the bright, tropical flowers. Brilliant parrots whistled at us from the jungle trees. This was truly a paradise!

"Let's not go back!" Ned said. His eyes looked like two flames. "Let's escape now!'

There was silence, as we all considered our escape. Then, we made our way toward the beach, listening to Ned's argument.

Chapter

6

Cannibal
Island

Just as Ned was talking of escape, we stepped from the jungle. There on the beach stood Nemo! He was waiting with the boat to bring us back to the *Nautilus*. It was almost as if he knew what we were thinking!

I didn't want to argue with the captain, so I began to load the boat with the fresh food. Conseil quickly helped me.

But Ned raised his fists—ready to fight Nemo for his freedom! Just as the fight was about to begin, Ned backed away. A large stone had been thrown from the jungle, hitting Ned's fist!

In their surprise, Ned and the captain

forgot about fighting. We all looked towards the jungle.

"It must be a monkey," I said, feeling afraid.

A second stone knocked a coconut right out of Conseil's hand! We snatched our guns—ready to face the danger.

Out of the jungle came a rain of spears! A gang of screaming savages leaped onto the beach!

"Cannibals! Run for the boat!" Ned yelled.

We didn't need to be told twice! Conseil and I ran for our lives! We jumped into the boat, but saw that Ned and Nemo were not with us!

Ned would not get in the boat without the pig he had shot in the hunt! And Captain Nemo was risking his own life to help Ned carry the pig!

"The darned fool!" I yelled, "he's going to get us all killed for the sake of a pork dinner!"

Ned and the captain leaped for the boat. The cannibals were right behind them.

"Pull! Pull for your lives!" yelled Nemo as he grabbed the oars.

With all of us rowing, we moved quickly away from the beach. But the savages kept coming! There were at least a hundred of them!

The angry natives began to wade into the water after us!

"We're not going to make it!" panted Conseil.

"Just keep pulling!" roared the captain.

As I rowed, I got a good look at the natives.

They were very fierce. Their faces were painted like horrible masks. They wore bones stuck in their ears, noses—even their lips! The air was filled with the sound of wild screams.

These men must be the dreaded head-hunters who ate human flesh! In a shower of spears, arrows, and stones, we finally made it back to safety in the *Nautilus.*

Safe aboard the ship, we were able to relax. I was glad to be safe, but I was still very worried. Since the top deck of the ship was out of water, the natives might try to climb aboard.

"Don't you think that you should have some of your men guard the ship tonight?" I asked.

"Nonsense!" snorted the captain. "You have nothing to fear, Professor!"

I left Captain Nemo studying his maps and went up on deck. Conseil was there, and we stood and watched the shore. The beach blazed with the native's fires. They were watching us, and waiting...

I did not sleep well that night. I

dreamed of savages leaping on me with their raised spears!

At dawn, I hurried out on the deck. There were now five hundred cannibals gathered on the beach! I ran below to get Captain Nemo.

The captain went up on deck and looked at the screaming natives on shore.

"For the last time, you have nothing to worry about, Professor!" Captain Nemo said, sounding angry. "Now let me go study my maps!"

"But captain, perhaps you should at least close the hatches!" I begged.

"I want fresh air!" Nemo thundered.

The cannibals got into their canoes. Slowly, they paddled closer to the ship. As I watched, poisoned arrows filled the air. They were attacking!

I rushed inside the ship. Nemo was still looking at his maps. I said nothing to him. I was afraid he would get angry.

"The tide will rise in a half hour," he told me. "Then we can get away from here," he added.

Oh! If only the tide would hurry! I tried to help the captain with the maps. Then I heard something on deck! A second later, the face of a cannibal looked down from the hatch! He held a poisoned spear.

A shrunken head hung from the brown man's waist. It was a human head!

"Captain! We shall be killed!" I screamed.

Captain Nemo did not even look up from his maps! The savage began to climb down the ladder. I stood, frozen with fear.

Then the savage gave a terrible scream. Sparks flew from the ladder. The

ladder had given him a terrific shock. Still screaming, the native leaped up the ladder and jumped overboard. The rest of the cannibals paddled quickly to the shore and ran into the jungle. So, that's it! I thought. Nemo guards his ship with electric power!

Just then, the ship began to float on the rising tide. Soon the *Nautilus* was free

of the reef that had held her. We headed out to sea, safe once again. Captain Nemo had been right about everything!

After a couple of days, a storm approached. That did not bother the ship at all. The Nautilus went deep beneath the waves, where the water was as smooth as glass.

I was looking out the big window, and I saw that the ship was surrounded by very bright light. At first, I thought that the electric beams had been turned on. Then I saw that the light was made by millions of tiny, glowing sea creatures turning the dark water into beautiful liquid light!

After the storm, Captain Nemo took the *Nautilus* up to the surface. He stood looking through his telescope for a very long time. Then he hurried below to look at his maps. I followed him and stood trying to look over his shoulder, but the captain paid no attention to me. I went back up on deck, but I saw nothing on the ocean—only grey sea meeting grey sky.

I went back down to see what Nemo had been studying. I picked up a telescope, raising it to my eyes. Suddenly, it was yanked from my hand. Nemo was standing there shaking with anger!

"Professor!" he hissed. "There are

some things that you must *not know!*" Nemo called a guard. "Lock the Professor in his cabin!" he ordered.

When I arrived at my cabin, Ned and Conseil were there. We were all locked in together.

"Professor, what is happening?" asked Conseil.

"There is something that the captain does not want us to see!" I answered.

Just then, dinner was brought in for the three of us; we ate in worried silence.

"Whatever it is, Nemo is sure going to a lot of trouble to keep his secrets!" grumbled Ned.

A moment later, I looked up to answer, but Ned had fallen asleep! Conseil lay his head down on the table. Then I felt myself getting drowsy.

"We have been drugged!" I groaned.

Darkness came over me, and I could not speak or move!

Chapter

7

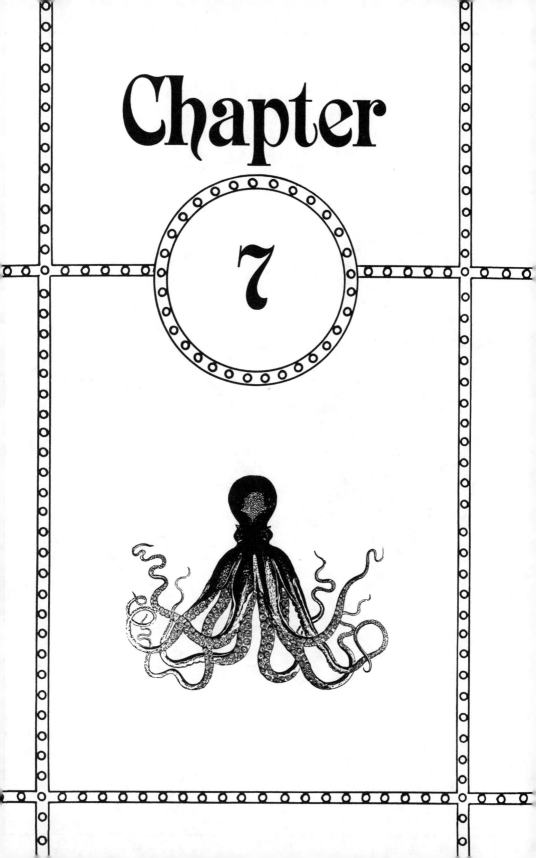

Shark Attack

The next morning, I woke up alone in my cabin. Ned and Conseil must have been carried away. I felt fine, but I wondered why the captain had drugged us. I went to the door of my cabin, and it was open. I was free to roam the ship.

Captain Nemo came to my door. His eyes were all red, and he looked very tired.

"I have a sick man on board," Nemo said with great sadness. "Can you help him?"

A young man lay on the bed. His head was wrapped in bandages that were soaked with blood. The wound was so deep that the poor man's brain was showing.

"There is nothing I can do. He is dying," I said. Captain Nemo's eyes filled with tears.

The young man died and was buried at sea. I did not see Captain Nemo for several days after that. I wondered over and over again how the young man had been so badly hurt.

We soon came to the crystal waters of the Indian Ocean. Nemo asked me to go diving with him for pearls. We got into our

diving suits, and soon we were on the bottom of that sparkling sea.

Nemo led the way to an undersea cave. It was dark and gloomy inside. The captain moved toward a large, white shape. It was a giant oyster that must

have weighed seven hundred pounds! Nemo forced open the shell. Inside was a glowing pearl the size of a coconut!

Once outside the cave, I saw a shadow in the water. It was an Indian pearl diver.

The water in which he swam was the

the clearest water in the world. From the surface, you could look down three hundred feet and see tiny crabs crawling on the bottom! The diver had no trouble spotting oysters.

This water was also filled with the biggest and meanest sharks in the seas! I was frightened, but I didn't say anything to Captain Nemo.

We watched the diver go to the bottom as he held his breath. He would grab an armload of oysters, then surface to his tiny boat. It was then that I saw another terrible shadow. It was a killer shark!

The shark was headed straight for the

poor diver! The jaws of the killer fish were open wide. Its eyes were dull and black.

The diver was able to move aside just in time to escape the shark's jaws, but he was hit in the chest by its powerful tail. The poor diver was knocked unconscious. He lay death-like on the ocean floor. Then the shark came back to make its kill!

Captain Nemo sprang into action. He

leaped at the fierce shark, armed with only a knife in his hand! The shark turned and headed right for Nemo! His gaping jaws looked as if they would cut the captain in two!

Captain Nemo braced himself. The man-killer came at him with the deadly speed of a freight train! Nemo side-stepped the shark with the grace of a dancer, but the killer turned and charged again. Nemo was ready.

As the shark made his next pass, Captain Nemo sank his knife deep into the belly of the shark!

Blood gushed from the shark's pale underside, and the water turned bright red. Soon there was so much blood in the water that I could not even see the captain! Behind the curtain of blood, raged the battle!

Then, there was a clear spot in the water. I saw the captain. He had the shark by the fins. Although Nemo had stabbed the shark over and over, he could not reach its heart. He was getting tired. Suddenly, he lost his grip!

The killer shark closed in on the weary captain. I was so afraid that I couldn't move a muscle in my body.

Then I remembered Ned's harpoon! I had taken it along for extra protection. I

rushed at the shark and plunged the harpoon in as deeply as it would go! I did not miss! The shark was struck right through the heart! Twisting in agony, it sank to the bottom. I had killed it!

Captain Nemo was unhurt. When we recovered, we remembered the Indian diver. Rushing to where the poor fellow lay, we found him still tied to the rock he used to help him sink to the bottom. We cut the helpless diver free and pulled him to safety.

We dragged the Indian into his tiny wooden boat. He looked pale and was barely breathing. His blue lips trembled, then they were still. The captain rubbed the man's chest to revive him.

The diver finally opened his eyes. In shock, he stared at our strange suits and big copper helmets. He was even more shocked when Captain Nemo took out a bag of shining pearls and put it in his hand! We left the Indian safe in his boat—with his precious bag of pearls.

Once back on the bottom, we looked

at the dead shark. He was huge with six rows of teeth!

Safe aboard the *Nautilus*, the captain and I rested from our battle with the shark. A day later, Captain Nemo called me to the library.

"I thank you with my heart, Professor," the captain said with great warmth and kindness. "You saved me from certain death."

"I was only paying you back for saving me! It was you who first pulled the three of us from the water," I reminded him.

He nodded and smiled.

Soon we entered the Red Sea. We saw

the spot where Moses was said to have parted the waters! We all watched our surroundings with great awe and wonder.

Then, one clear day, we saw something even more interesting—and very much alive!

The *Nautilus* was cruising along on the surface, cutting the water like a knife. Ned and I were talking on deck, enjoying very much the open air. Suddenly, we saw a huge, black shape in the water.

"Maybe it's a rocky island," I suggested to Ned.

He didn't reply, but stared in wonder.

"Maybe it's a whale!" Ned said at last,

his eyes eager and full of excitement. "Are there any whales in the Red Sea?"

"It's not a whale," I answered, straining to finally name the mysterious creature.

We were nearing the animal now. I began to see it more clearly, and then I knew exactly what it was. My heart raced. I turned to Ned, and slapped his on the back.

"My word, Ned, it's a dugong!" I exclaimed.

"What on earth is a dugong?" asked Ned.

"It is a rare sea animal found only in this part of the world," I explained.

Ned ran to the side of the deck and stood staring at the huge animal.

"Is it dangerous?" he asked.

"Not very. And I hear it tastes better than steak!" I told him.

That did it! Ned got a very hungry look on his face. He ran to get his harpoon.

Chapter

8

The Dugong

Captain Nemo stepped out onto the deck just as Ned was running to get his harpoon. Ned bumped into the captain and knocked him down!

I thought Nemo would be furious, but he got up smiling, turning to face a worried Ned.

"What's your hurry?" the captain asked.

"That!" exclaimed Ned, pointing to the dugong, "I wanted to get my harpoon!"

"So you would like a hunt?" said Captain Nemo.

He called to some of his sailors. Soon they came on deck with harpoons. The rowboat was put into the water and made ready for the hunt. Ned jumped into the rowboat taking a place in the front; Conseil and I sat in the back.

The rowboat was ready to push away from the ship, but the captain did not get in.

"Aren't you coming, captain?" I asked him.

"No" he replied, "but I wish you good luck!"

We pushed off and headed towards the floating dugong. The oars were silent as they sliced the water. We crept up close to the huge creature and took a good look at it. It was about thirty feet long! Two very long, pointed teeth stuck out of its mouth. The dugong looked more dangerous close up than it had from the ship!

Ned stood ready to throw his harpoon. Just as the harpoon left his hand,

the dugong hissed and dove under the water.

"A thousand devils!" groaned Ned.

"You wounded it!" cried Conseil. "Look at all the blood in the water!"

We chased the wounded animal for an hour, and Ned was getting very angry that we couldn't catch it. All of a sudden the huge beast charged right at our little boat!

The boat almost turned over. It was flooded with gallons of water! For a second, we forgot the dugong and tried to bail out our sinking boat.

All of us were working to keep the boat afloat —all except Ned. He was trying his hardest to kill the mighty dugong. He

stood tall and firm, sinking his harpoon into the creature again and again. But the dugong would not die!

I heard the teeth of the beast grinding on the boat. Then to our horror, the giant animal lifted our boat right out of the water!

We were falling all over each other, but nobody could do anything to stop the dugong. Ned stood up, fighting to keep his balance. He threw his harpoon with the last of his strength. His aim was perfect! The dugong had been pierced right through the heart! We all cheered.

With a groan, the dying animal sank. The huge dugong was dead at last. Back we went to the *Nautilus*, towing Ned's prize catch behind us.

That night at dinner, we were served the most delicious meal we had ever eaten! The tasty, roasted dugong was better than either steak or candy. Ned was the hero of the day, and we all drank a toast to him.

The next day, late in the afternoon, I

joined Captain Nemo at the lookout. We saw the sun setting behind steep, rocky cliffs, and we seemed to be heading straight for them!

"What are we doing?" I asked, a bit afraid.

"We are heading for the secret Arabian tunnel. Those cliffs mark the entrance, and I am the only one who knows where it is!" said Nemo.

"Do you mean the tunnel is under water?" I asked him.

"Get below!" ordered the captain, " the ship is about to go under."

That answered my question! The captain himself would steer the Nautilus through the narrow tunnel. Down into the dark tunnel we went. The rock walls closed in on us!

All at once, a strong current grabbed the ship, and we shot through the tunnel like a bullet.

Out of the window, I could see the ruins of an ancient city. It was the lost continent of Atlantis! I could almost see

the ghostly robes of forgotten kings drifting in the current.

The next day, I was reading on a couch near the big window. All of a sudden, I began to feel very hot. I looked at the thermometer on the wall. It read one hundred degrees!

I could see that the water was white and bubbly outside the ship. The sea itself was boiling! I touched the window by mistake, and it burned my hand!

Just then, Captain Nemo walked in and looked out.

"How would you like to see an under-water volcano?" he asked.

"If we won't be boiled to death out there!" I exclaimed.

"Our diving suits will protect us," he promised me.

Once we were outside the ship, the water began to turn a flaming red. Soon the volcano started to erupt. It was a beautiful and a terrible sight at the same time. I was amazed by the power of nature!

Before long, I began to sweat inside my suit. I felt as if I were being cooked alive! Captain Nemo must have felt the same, because he gave a sign to return to the ship.

Again aboard the *Nautilus*, the captain ordered the engines to be started at once. Going at top speed, we left the fiery waters behind. Soon, we were cruising through cool, crystal waters once more.

Chapter

9

The South Pole

It was not long before we came to the great Atlantic Ocean. The *Nautilus* was now cruising near Spain. I was not surprised when Ned came to me with another plan of escape.

"Professor, now is our chance!" Ned whispered. "We are close enough to friendly nations to make a break for it!" he pleaded.

"When shall we try our luck?" I asked Ned.

"Tonight!" he answered. "At dark, I will steal the rowboat," Ned said quickly. Then he left.

I did not know what to do! I did want

my freedom, but I hated to leave the wonderful *Nautilus*, where I was seeing and learning so much. I hid in my cabin so I would not have to face Captain Nemo.

I was still in my cabin, when I felt a sharp bump. The *Nautilus* had stopped! I raced out of my room and up onto the deck. The late afternoon sun was gleaming brightly on some wrecked ships.

Then I saw what was making such a golden glow. Chests filled with gold and jewels were spilled open on the decks of the ships!

"These are the famous treasure ships of Spain!" Captain Nemo told me. "And this is the secret reef where they were wrecked," he said.

"Are you the only one who knows this place?" I asked Nemo.

"Yes!" he exclaimed, " and I am a billionaire!"

"What will you do with all that money?"

"I will send it to the poor people of the earth," Nemo answered me quietly.

What a kind man Captain Nemo was—powerful, yet kind! But we would not be able to escape tonight—Nemo's men were everywhere. Ned would be very disappointed.

We went at top speed for many days without stopping. It was almost as if Captain Nemo were making sure that we would never be able to escape! One day, I saw something shining brightly in the distance. When the ship got closer, I saw huge mountains of ice!

"No one has ever made it to the South

Pole alive!" Nemo exclaimed, "I will be the *first!*"

I wondered then if the captain was crazy. Other men had tried to reach the

South Pole— and all of them had died trying!

In spite of being worried, I found this place very beautiful. Ice mountains sparkled and were strung with glowing rainbows; floating icebergs were like crystal castles shining in the sun. Captain Nemo steered the *Nautilus* carefully among the giant ice forms. Day after day, the ship inched along a narrow, winding path between the ice. Often, the ship squeezed through with only inches to spare!

It was very cold. The thermometer stayed below zero, and it was daylight all the time. Sometimes there were great avalanches of ice that fell with crushing force.

The tiny paths between the ice began to get even narrower, and soon the *Nautilus* faced giant sheets of solid ice. But that did not stop Captain Nemo—or his powerful ship!

The captain drove his ship forward at full power. The *Nautilus* rammed her way through the ice, making her own path!

Day after day, the sturdy ship broke

the ice with terrible cracking sounds. Huge chunks of ice flew into the air and struck the ship like giant hailstones. In that cold and lonely sea, Nemo pushed on toward the South Pole.

One freezing day, the *Nautilus* could

not move forward. The ice was piled two hundred feet high in front of the ship. We were trapped!

In an hour, the ship was becoming frozen in the thick ice. I looked out into the distance. All I could see was miles and miles of deserted ice. I was sure that we would never make it to the South Pole. I was afraid that we were stuck forever!

"What are we going to do?" I aked the captain. "We are trapped in this land of ice!"

"Trapped? Never!" boomed the captain. "If we can't go around or through— we'll go under!"

Captain Nemo was right. After a dark

journey under the ice, we reached open water. Then we sighted land. The search for the South Pole began. Would we be the first to find it?

We set off across the glittering ice. It was like a fairyland! Tall towers of ice pointed at the sky; snow made swirling patterns on the ground.

We saw white birds and gentle seals. We lived on penguin eggs and walrus meat, wrapping the skins around our feet for warmth.

It began to snow. Our heavy clothes made it hard to walk, and we would get very tired in a short time.

One day the mist cleared, and we saw a mountain peak. Inch by inch, we struggled to the top. Captain Nemo took out his compass.

"This is it!" Nemo cried, "The South Pole!"

Nemo planted the black and gold flag of the *Nautilus* on the mountaintop.

"I have discovered the South Pole!" the captain cried. 'We are the first to set foot on this place!"

We bowed our head while Captain Nemo claimed the land for himelf.

"May the sun shine forever on my new land," the captain exclaimed.

On the way back to the ship, I had a sad thought. Captain Nemo had discovered the South Pole, but the rest of the world might never know that he did.

Chapter

10

Giant
Squid

We soon left the South Pole and headed north. It was not long before we came to the warm waters of the Caribbean Sea.

I spent a lot of time looking out of the big window. Colorful creatures gave life to the clear turquoise water. It was like watching a carnival.

One day, the ship began to dive down much deeper than usual. The *Nautilus* went down to a depth of twenty thousand feet before it stopped.

Ned and I were looking out at the dark waters. There were forests of thick seaweed and great underwater caves.

Suddenly, we saw the seaweed begin to wiggle and squirm.

"Maybe it's a monster!" Ned joked.

"This is a good place for monsters!" I laughed.

As I turned to the window, my laughter caught in my throat. The huge, bulging eyes of a giant squid were staring in at me! The captain ran in to take a look at the horrible creature.

"We're in for trouble!" Nemo said,

looking very worried. "They're holding the ship! Soon we won't be able to move!" Nemo explained, running for the controls.

Soon, *seven* deadly squid had taken hold of the ship! They were so ugly, it made me weak to look at them! The creatures were twenty-five feet long and

weighed about fifty thousand pounds!
They each had eight tentacles with hun-
dreds of suckers on them. Their mouths
were like giant beaks, and their tongues
had rows of sharp teeth!

Captain Nemo raised the ship to the
surface. We would fight the giant squid off

with axes, swords, and Ned's trusty harpoon.

A sailor started to open the hatch, but it was torn right off its hinges! Like a huge snake, a tentacle came down and grabbed the poor sailor!

It was a horrible thing to watch! He was choking and screaming for help. I shall never forget his helpless cries.

Nemo tried to save his man, but the squid dragged him down headfirst into the churning waters and up again. We all attacked the creature with great fury. The axes cut deep slits in its jellylike flesh. Black liquid spurted from the squid's mouth. The air was filled with a dreadful stink, and the deck was slippery with slime.

The squid still held the sailor in the only tentacle it had left—Nemo had cut off all the others! It looked like Nemo might

save his sailor, but suddenly, the squid slithered off the deck and carried the doomed sailor to the bottom of the sea!

One by one, the squid slipped into the sea. The deck was a slimy mixture of red blood and stinking, black liquid.

Captain Nemo stood staring at the sea. His uniform was ripped, and he was covered with blood. Tears of great sorrow rolled down the poor captain's face.

This was the second man that Nemo had lost on this voyage, and this poor sailor had died so horribly! He had been choked, then drowned in the dark waters. The poor sailor would never rest peacefully in the quiet gardens of the sea. His life had been torn from him in a terrible way as he tried to fight for his captain.

Nemo could not forget the awful scene. He was tortured by the sailor's final cries. He stayed in his cabin the rest of that day. The *Nautilus* just drifted slowly along, floating in the cold and lonely sea.

Chapter

11

A Fight to the Finish

The *Nautilus* drifted north, carried along by the swift current of the Gulf Stream. Captain Nemo did not leave his cabin. He seemed to care no longer about his ship. He felt that the sea had turned against him.

Before long, the *Nautilus* began to drift closer to the shores of America. Again Ned saw the chance for an escape!

There were a lot of boats on the American coast, and Ned was sure that one of them would pick us up. But his plans were ruined. The weather turned stormy. Cyclones whipped the waves into a frenzy. It would be certain death to try and escape in that kind of weather—with waves as big as mountains!

However, Ned had made up his mind that he was going to try and escape.

Conseil and I sat down with him to talk things over.

"I can't stand this any longer!" shouted Ned. "I want to go back to my home and family!"

"What can we do?" I asked. "You know that the captain said we can never leave!"

"Ask him again!" Ned shouted, "I do not want to be a prisoner for the rest of my life!"

I decided to try to reason with Captain Nemo. Soon, Ned would do something foolish and endanger his life. I had little hope of convincing the captain to let us go. But surely, there was some way.

I found Captain Nemo playing the organ in his cabin. He turned around to face me.

"What do you want!" he said rudely. "I am busy! Leave me alone!" he raged.

I knew that this was not a good time to speak to Nemo, but I didn't care. Bravely, I stood before him, squaring my shoulders.

"Captain, I must speak to you!" I said firmly.

Nemo stood thinking. He looked as though he didn't hear me. Then he pointed to a book.

"This is my diary," he said. "It tells my life story and all my secrets."

The secrets of the great Captain Nemo! I could hardly believe my ears! Then I got an idea.

"Captain, let me and my friends take care of that diary for you!" I said. "Think of what the world could do with your knowledge!" I exclaimed.

"Now I see what you want!" screamed

Nemo. "Never! Never! You will never leave the *Nautilus* alive!"

When I told Ned and Conseil what Nemo had said, Ned turned pale and clenched his fists.

"We will leave this ship no matter what Nemo says!" Ned swore.

But the storm pushed the *Nautilus* away from the United States. We had missed our chance! Ned felt so upset—he just stayed in his cabin.

The next day, the storm cleared. We were very far north. Ned and I went out on the deck. I tried to cheer him up. Then we saw a ship! It was way off in the distance, but it was headed right towards us!

"What kind of ship is that?" I asked Ned.

"Why, it's a warship!" Ned cried excitedly.

Ned was really joyous. He thought that the warship would pick us up if we could get off the *Nautilus*. All at once there was a loud bang. Then we heard a big splash.

"What was that!?" I asked Ned.

"It was a cannon ball!" Ned shouted, "they're firing at us!" He waved his hand-kerchief at the ship as a sign of peace.

Suddenly, Captain Nemo sprang up on deck and knocked Ned flat!

"You fool!" the captain screamed, "I'll nail you to the deck if you try that again!"

Ned didn't say a word, he just slunk below. The captain looked like a madman! His face was white, and his black eyes looked like burning coals. I stood watching as Nemo raged.

I remembered another time when Captain Nemo was very nasty–the night he had locked us in the cabin and drugged us. Then, there was the poor sailor who had died from terrible head wounds. All at once I knew. Captain Nemo

was at war with the world! He was the enemy!

Captain Nemo hoisted the black and gold flag of the *Nautilus*. He was getting his mighty ship ready for battle!

"Why are you going to attack?" I shouted at Nemo. "You can easily dive and get away!"

"I am going to sink that ship!" Nemo roared, pacing back and forth like an angry animal.

"I have lost my country, my wife, and my children!" the captain cried. "That ship is everything that I hate! I will destroy it!"

Then Nemo became quiet. He stood staring.

The rest of that day, Nemo let the warship chase the *Nautilus*. He kept the warship in his sights, but he stayed out of firing range.

I hurried to find Ned and Conseil. The three of us ducked into my cabin.

"We have *got* to escape!" I whispered "Captain Nemo is a madman!"

"Good!" said Ned, "we'll try it at night-fall!"

Night came. Up on deck, Nemo stood there watching the warship in the moon-light.

It was getting closer. I could see the shadows of her crew running about on the deck. The warship was going at top speed. The glow fom her engines colored her red. Sparks leaped into the air and fell like dying stars.

Captain Nemo stood watching...and waiting. A misty dawn broke over the deadly chase. As the sun began to rise, the *Nautilus* started to slow down. Nemo was letting the warship catch up!

"This is it!" I said to Ned and Conseil.

The three of us waited in the salon by the big window. With pounding hearts, we waited to see what would happen!

The *Nautilus* dove down, just under the surface of the water. The warship wouldn't even know what was attacking it!

All at once, the *Nautilus* charged. It charged with powerful engines going full blast. It was going so fast, that we were flattened against the wall. Then came the horrible sound of ripping metal. I shall never forget it!

The *Nautilus* went right through the warship as easily as a sharp knife goes through butter. The great bulk of the warship began to sink—with all hands aboard!

It was an awful sight! Water poured like great rivers into the wounded warship. As the water rose, the poor men struggled to hold onto anything they could find. One hundred men were drowning before our eyes!

After cutting through the ship, Captain Nemo went above, and I followed. He just stood there watching! The drowning men must have taken their last gulps

of air before the water filled their screaming mouths.

Then there was a terrible explosion.
My eyes bulged in horror as I saw the warship plunge to the bottom of the sea!

I turned toward Captain Nemo. So
this was his kind of justice! I no longer
cared about myself. I would tell him what
I thought. He was a murderer!

Before I could speak, Captain Nemo
went below. I followed him to his salon,
where he fell on his knees. He stretched
his arms toward a small painting of a
woman and two children. Then the great
Nemo hung his head and began to sob.

Chapter

12

Good-bye,
Captain Nemo

After that terrible incident with the warship, Captain Nemo didn't come out of his cabin. The ship sped north through the cold mists. No one seemed to be running the ship. No one seemed to care.

One morning Ned came to me. We both knew it was time to escape. "We can try to make it in the rowboat," Ned said. "But the sea is very rough."

"Then we'll die together trying!" I swore.

I heard the captain playing the organ. The wailing music sounded like the crying of a lost soul. Ned, Conseil, and I found the rowboat. We were ready to escape.

Just as we were getting in, we heard loud shouts coming from the crew.

"The maelstrom!" the sailors cried.

The maelstrom was a giant whirlpool from which no ship had ever escaped! The whirlpool swallowed everything that got caught in it: ships, whales, and even polar bears were sucked into the sea forever!

"Row! Row! Row like the devil!" shouted Ned.

We broke away from the *Nautilus* and began to row with all our strength. Ned was pulling furiously.

The *Nautilus* spun like a top as she struggled for survival. I watched the ship

strain against the force of the maelstrom. There was a roaring louder than thunder! I gave my oar a mighty pull, but I slipped back and hit my head. I felt myself beginning to faint!

I woke up in the house of a kindly fisherman. Ned and Conseil were by my side. We were all well! In great joy, I hugged my two friends.

We were safe in Norway, and the Norwegians would send Conseil and me to France; Ned would go home to Canada. Home again!

But what about Captain Nemo? None of us saw what happened to the *Nautilus*. Had the mighty ship surived the maelstrom? Did her great captain still roam the oceans of the world?

With Captain Nemo, I had seen wonders that no man had ever seen. I had

been shown the marvelous secrets of the deep. But who was Captain Nemo: a devil? A hero? Whoever he was, I would never forget him!

"Captain Nemo, I salute you!" I cried to the blue, sparkling sea. "I wish you peace!"

THE END

ABOUT THE AUTHOR

JULES VERNE was born in 1828 in Nantes, France. Following a family tradition of sea-faring, young Verne tried to run away from home and work as a cabin boy on a ship. However, he was stopped and returned to his parents.

His family later sent him to Paris to study law. In Paris, however, Verne became interested in the theater and started writing plays. When his parents cut off his allowance, Verne started writing stories to earn his living.

Soon Verne was turning out fantastic stories, inspired by all the scientific discoveries made at the time. His works include *Journey to the Center of the Earth*, *20,000 Leagues Under the Sea*, and *Around the World in Eighty Days*.

Verne's books made him famous and rich. He bought a yacht and wrote as he sailed from port to port. He died in 1905 in Amiens, France.

The Young Collector's
Illustrated Classics

Adventures of Robin Hood
Black Beauty
Call of the Wild
Dracula
Frankenstein
Heidi
Little Women
Moby Dick
Oliver Twist
Peter Pan
The Prince and the Pauper
The Secret Garden
Swiss Family Robinson
Treasure Island
20,000 Leagues Under the Sea
White Fang